7000346209

D1380563

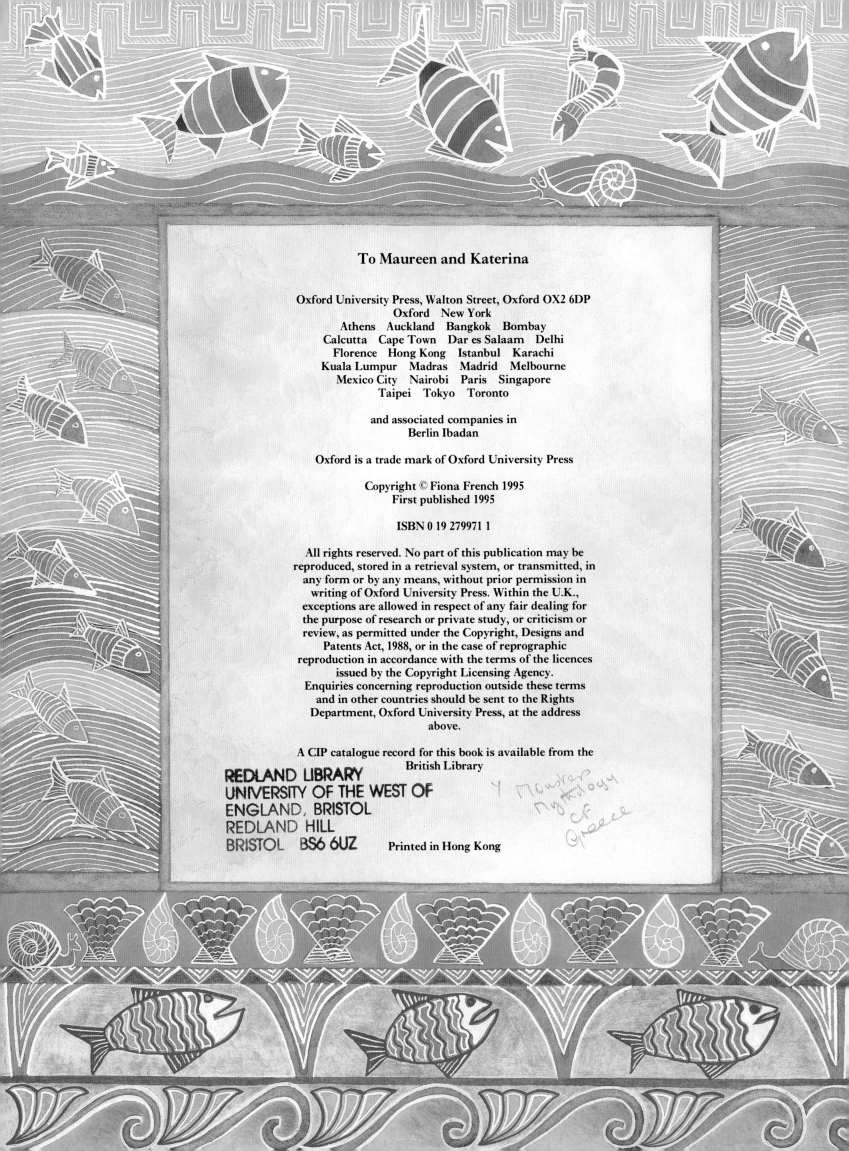

To Maureen and Katerina

Oxford University Press, Walton Street, Oxford OX2 6DP
Oxford   New York
Athens   Auckland   Bangkok   Bombay
Calcutta   Cape Town   Dar es Salaam   Delhi
Florence   Hong Kong   Istanbul   Karachi
Kuala Lumpur   Madras   Madrid   Melbourne
Mexico City   Nairobi   Paris   Singapore
Taipei   Tokyo   Toronto

and associated companies in
Berlin Ibadan

Oxford is a trade mark of Oxford University Press

Copyright © Fiona French 1995
First published 1995

ISBN 0 19 279971 1

All rights reserved. No part of this publication may be
reproduced, stored in a retrieval system, or transmitted, in
any form or by any means, without prior permission in
writing of Oxford University Press. Within the U.K.,
exceptions are allowed in respect of any fair dealing for
the purpose of research or private study, or criticism or
review, as permitted under the Copyright, Designs and
Patents Act, 1988, or in the case of reprographic
reproduction in accordance with the terms of the licences
issued by the Copyright Licensing Agency.
Enquiries concerning reproduction outside these terms
and in other countries should be sent to the Rights
Department, Oxford University Press, at the address
above.

A CIP catalogue record for this book is available from the
British Library

REDLAND LIBRARY
UNIVERSITY OF THE WEST OF
ENGLAND, BRISTOL
REDLAND HILL
BRISTOL BS6 6UZ

Printed in Hong Kong

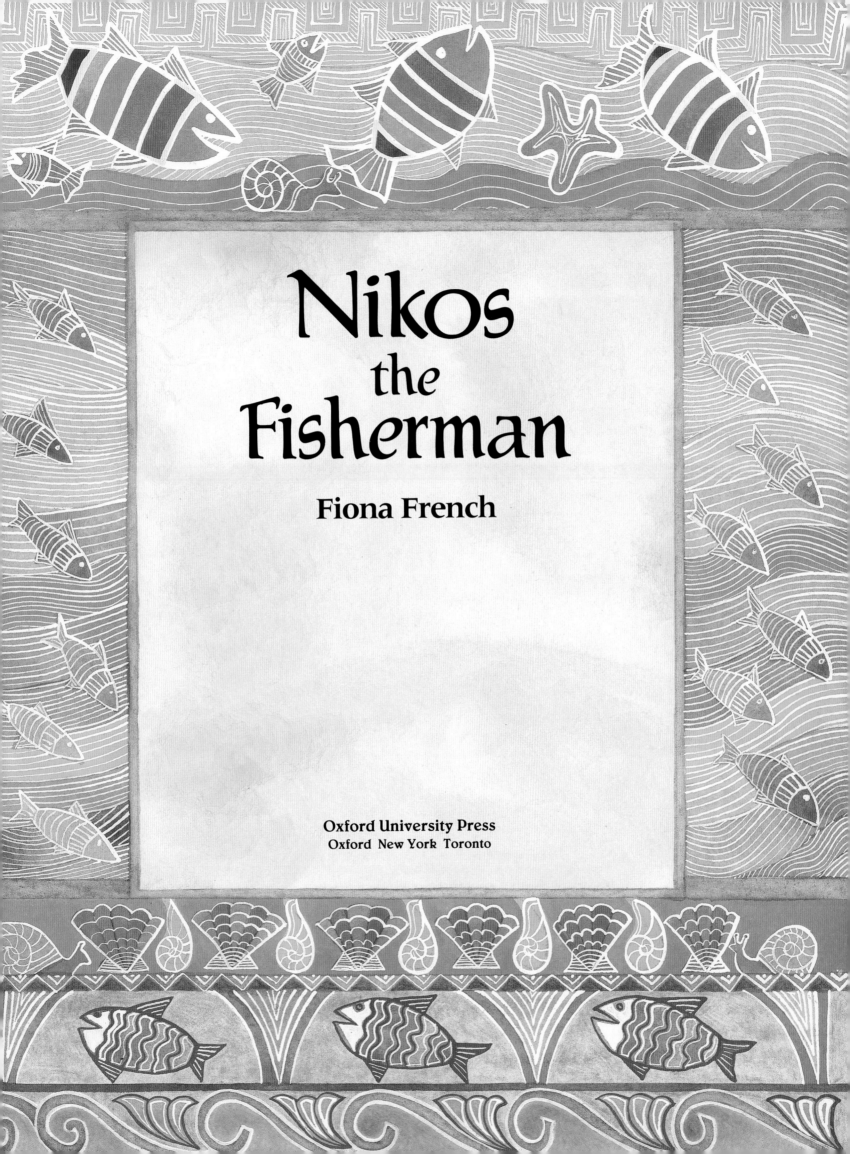

Nikos
the
Fisherman

Fiona French

Oxford University Press
Oxford New York Toronto

NIKOS THE FISHERMAN lived in a small village
on a beautiful Greek island.
He had a fishing boat called *Aphrodite*.
Every day he sailed out to sea to catch fish
and every evening he sold his catch on
the seashore.

One day, Nikos sailed much further out to sea
and a fierce storm overtook him.
The mountainous waves nearly overturned
his boat.
Nikos was very frightened.
'Aphrodite, please help me,'
he whispered.

At that moment the storm died away
and the little boat was washed up
on the shores of a strange island.
Nearby, a beautiful girl sat on a rock.
She was weeping and trying to escape
from heavy chains.

'I'll undo those for you,' said Nikos.
He fetched some steel-cutters from his
boat and set her free.

Suddenly a huge monster rose out of the sea.
'Where's my dinner?' it roared.
Nikos stood on a small rock and
shouted to the monster,
'If you let the girl go, I will give you some
delicious fish to eat and some baklava
for pudding.'
'Yummy,' said the sea monster.
'I was getting tired of the same thing every day.'

'Thank you for setting me free,' said the girl,
and she ran off up the steep hillside.
'Wait a minute,' cried Nikos.
'Who are you? Where am I?
What is this place?'
The girl did not hear him.
She ran faster and faster.

Nikos ran after her.
'What is your name?' he puffed.
'My name is Ariadne,' she called
as she ran into a deep, dark cavern.

Too late, Nikos realized they were
in the dark labyrinth, and galloping out of the
darkness came the dreadful Minotaur.

'At last,' roared the Minotaur.
'Here's my dinner.'
'Wait!' cried Nikos. 'On my boat is a
dish of moussaka just cooked and
ready to eat and there is baklava for pudding.'
'How nice,' said the Minotaur.
'That will make a change from eating humans.'

'Follow me,' said Ariadne.
'I know the way.' And she led
them out of the labyrinth.
But they had not gone far when
a thick grey mist swirled
around them.

'Ah, visitors!' cried the Gorgon.
'Dinner time again.'
All the snakes on her head swished
with pleasure.
'Yes, yes. Visitors, visitors,' they said.
'Oh, what is the good,' she sighed, glumly.
'I always turn them to stone, and I'm so hungry.'
'Stones, stones. So hungry. So hungry,' chorused
the snakes.

'If I give you my sunglasses to wear,'
said Nikos, 'you won't glare at everything,
you'll be much more friendly.
Why don't you join us all for a feast?'
'A feast, a feast. How nice, how nice,'
said the snakes.

'What a good idea,' said the Gorgon.
'I will bring a bottle of wine.'
'Retsina, retsina,' hissed the snakes joyfully.
She put on the sunglasses and led the way
down the cliffs back to the little boat on the
seashore.

The hungry sea monster was waiting
for them, and they all gathered round
and ate fried squid for starters,
with moussaka to follow, and,
of course, baklava for pudding.
'I must learn to cook,' said the Gorgon.
'Yes, yes. Must, must,' said the snakes.

Nikos invited Ariadne for a holiday on his island. They were quite sad when the time came to leave, but everyone helped to push the little boat into the sea.

Waving happily to their friends on the seashore,
Nikos and Ariadne sailed away into the sunset,
back to the village on the beautiful Greek island.